THE SOCCER MOM FROM OUTER SPACE

From: Sophiascherr

To: Miss Kramer

Your **Wish** is granted.

With love to Joyce Weiner and Susan Peas,
two wonderfully inspirational cheerleading
soccer moms!

A special thanks to Lily and Arthur for being such
great sports while I worked on this book!
Love, Dad

Published by Dell Dragonfly Books, an imprint of Random House Children's Books
a division of Random House, Inc.
1540 Broadway, New York, New York 10036

Copyright © 2000 by Barney Saltzberg

Visit us on the Web! www.randomhouse.com/kids
Educators and librarians, for a variety of teaching tools, visit us at
www.randomhouse.com/teachers

Library of Congress Cataloging-in-Publication Data

Saltzberg, Barney.
The soccer mom from outer space / by Barney Saltzberg.
p. cm.
Summary: The night before Lena's first soccer game, her father tells her a story about how
his mother used to act bizarre at his soccer games and embarrass him.
[1. Soccer—Fiction. 2. Parent and child—Fiction.] I. Title.
PZ7.S1552So 2000
[E]—dc21
99-045414
ISBN 0-517-80063-2 (trade)
0-517-80064-0 (lib. bdg.)
0-440-41758-9 (pbk.)

Reprinted by arrangement with Crown Publishers

Printed in the United States of America
June 2002

10 9 8 7 6 5 4 3 2

THE SOCCER MOM FROM OUTER SPACE

BY BARNEY SALTZBERG

Dell Dragonfly Books
New York

The night before Lena played her first soccer game, her father said it was time he told her the true story of the soccer mom from outer space.

"Is this going to be like the time you told me the true story of the tap-dancing potato that comes if the tooth fairy is on vacation?" Lena asked.

"Not exactly," said her father. "This is a story about a boy named Ruben and his mom, Mrs. Drinkwater."

"Hey!" said Lena. "This is about you and Grandma!"

"No," her father laughed, "it's a story about *another* boy named Ruben Drinkwater and *his* mom!"

When Ruben Drinkwater joined the Atomic Pickles soccer team, his mom started acting as if she were from outer space! Ruben had never thought of his mom as an alien before. After all, he had known her since he was born.

If his mom were green with two heads and tentacles, he would have noticed.

It would have been hard to miss if she walked through walls or communicated with the head alien back on her home planet through a toaster.

At Ruben's first soccer game, his mom started out pretty quiet — a little "WOO!" here and a little "WOO!" there. He didn't really pay much attention.

But sometime during the second half, while Ruben was dribbling
the ball down the field, Mrs. Drinkwater started screaming.
She sounded like a human siren.

WOO-WOO-WOO-WOOOOOOOO!

When Ruben realized that his mom was making
all that noise, he tripped and fell on the grass.

"I've never seen you act like that before," Ruben said later.

"It was an exciting game!" said Mrs. Drinkwater.

"It was embarrassing!" Ruben told her.

"Oh, honey," she said, "don't be embarrassed. Everyone falls down."

Ruben decided his mom was acting as if she came from outer space because it was his first game. He figured she'd calm down by the next time he played.

The following week, Mrs. Drinkwater came to the game wearing a giant pickle hat. "Isn't this great?"

"What are my friends going to say when they see it?" Ruben asked.

"Oh, they'll have to get their *own* hats!" his mom answered.

Before Ruben could tell her that he didn't think anyone would want to wear a hat like hers, she started cheering. "My son Ruben's number four. He can kick and he can score! Go, Pickles!"

When the game was over, Mrs. Drinkwater skipped across the field.

Ruben watched his mom closely during the week. *She's acting like her old, normal self,* he thought. *There is definitely something about my soccer games that makes her act like an alien.*

Ruben was right. His mom came to the next game looking like a giant cheerleading pickle.

Everyone stared at her.

"Mom!" Ruben whined. "None of the other parents are dressed like you!"

"Oh, I know, honey!" Mrs. Drinkwater said. "Not everyone is as fortunate as you are!"

Before Ruben could say anything else, his mom started shouting:

EVERYBODY UP. GET ON YOUR FEET.

THE ATOMIC PICKLES CAN'T BE BEAT!

Then Ruben heard voices chanting over and over:

GO, PICKLES,
MEAN AND GREEN,
BEST BALLPLAYERS
YOU'VE EVER SEEN!

"How would you feel if I came to your office and acted like a cheerleader?" Ruben said to his mom after the game.

"Great idea, honey!" said Mrs. Drinkwater. "I could make you a little outfit and you could dress up like a computer!"

That night, Ruben found his mom practicing her cheerleading in the hall.

"I wanted to surprise you!" said Mrs. Drinkwater.

"That's okay!" Ruben told her. "I don't want any more surprises. In fact, all I want is for you to stop acting like the soccer mom from outer space!"

"Do you think that just because I get excited when you play soccer, I'm an alien?" Mrs. Drinkwater asked.

"You sure act like one at my games!" said Ruben.

"I suppose I could stop if that's what you really want," Mrs. Drinkwater said.

Ruben looked relieved. "Okay!"

"Are you *sure* you want me to stop?" his mom asked.

"Yes," he said, "I'm sure!"

"Are you *really* sure?" Mrs. Drinkwater asked him again.

"Yes," said Ruben, "I'm really sure!"

"Are you *really, really*—"

"MOM!" Ruben shouted. "I just want you to act like the other parents!"

"Okay," said Mrs. Drinkwater. "If that's what you want."

When they got to his next game, none of the other parents were there yet.

The Atomic Pickles stared at Ruben's mom.

The coach wanted to know where her pickle outfit was.

"I asked her not to wear it," Ruben told him.

"But she's our biggest fan!" one of the Atomic Pickles moaned.

"My mom?" asked Ruben. "Don't you think she acts like the soccer mom from outer space?"

"Of course we do!" the whole team shouted.

"The more your mom cheers," the coach said, "the better the team plays!"

Just then, Ruben saw what looked like a giant green spaceship coming in their direction. *Maybe my mom really is an alien!* Ruben thought for a second.

"It's a blimp!" the coach shouted.

The team cheered at the sight of their parents dressed as giant cheerleading pickles, waving pom-poms, inside the blimp.

Ruben laughed. "I guess I did say I wanted you to be like the other parents..."

"That's good!" said his mom. "Now we can all act like we're aliens and you won't be embarrassed anymore!"

Then Ruben, his mom, and the rest of the Atomic Pickles joined in as dozens of giant pickles danced across the field, chanting:

A SOCCER MOM. A SOCCER DAD.

IT'S NOT SO WEIRD. IT'S NOT SO BAD.

YOU SEE THEM CHEERING EVERYPLACE.

THEY ACT LIKE THEY'RE FROM OUTER SPACE!

"And that," said Lena's father, "is the true story of the soccer mom from outer space."

"I liked this story better than the one about the tap-dancing potato!" said Lena. "But I don't think anyone's parents would act so weird just because of a soccer game!"

"Well," said Lena's father, "you'd be surprised! But right now I think you should get some sleep, since tomorrow's your big day."

The next morning, Lena was ready for her first soccer game.

And so was her family!